Note to parents

This book is specially designed to share with preschool children.
Simple games and engaging illustrations prompt discussion and guide your child from one activity
to the next, introducing basic numeracy skills in a reassuring and playful way.

It is important to go at your child's own pace. There's plenty to entertain and stimulate in the
illustrations alone, and at first your child may just enjoy looking at the pictures and talking about them.
Draw your child's attention to the numbers on the pages. Point to and count the objects in the pictures.
This helps develop observational skills and introduces the language of numbers. Help familiarize your
child with the shape and sequence of numbers by using the number line at the bottom of each page.
Point to the numbers in sequence and say them out loud with your child.

The activities in this book provide a comprehensive look at numbers one to ten, and present
counting in a variety of ways. When your child is comfortable with these basic concepts, move on to
more challenging ones, such as pairing, sorting, and matching. Remember to offer lots of praise and
encouragement. As your child grows more confident, and inquisitive, use the section at the back
of the book to introduce the idea of numbers in everyday life.

Above all, enjoy sharing in your child's discovery of numbers. Your help and involvement will enable your
child to build the foundations of a firm understanding of numbers—and will also make learning fun!

Copyright © Alan Baker 1996, 2019
Text copyright © Kate Petty 1998
Consultant: Ann Montague-Smith

First published 1999 in the United States by Kingfisher
This edition published 2019 by Kingfisher
175 Fifth Ave., New York, NY 10010
Kingfisher is an imprint of Macmillan Children's Books, London
All rights reserved.

Library of Congress Cataloging-in-Publication data has been applied for

Distributed in the U.S. and Canada by Macmillan,
175 Fifth Ave., New York, NY 10010

For more information please visit www.kingfisherbooks.com

ISBN: 978-0-7534-7406-8

Printed in China
9 8 7 6 5 4 3 2 1
1TR/0919/WKT/UG/128MA

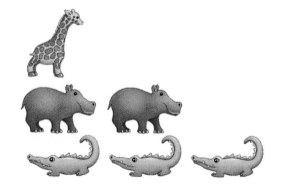

LITTLE RABBITS

FIRST NUMBERS

ALAN BAKER

Text by Kate Petty

KINGFISHER

LONDON & NEW YORK

Count to ten

1 one bear

2 two slippers

3 three ducks

6 six blocks

7 seven cookies

1 **2** **3** **4** **5**

4 four hats

5 five presents

8 eight strawberries

9 nine books

10 ten bubbles

Count the animals

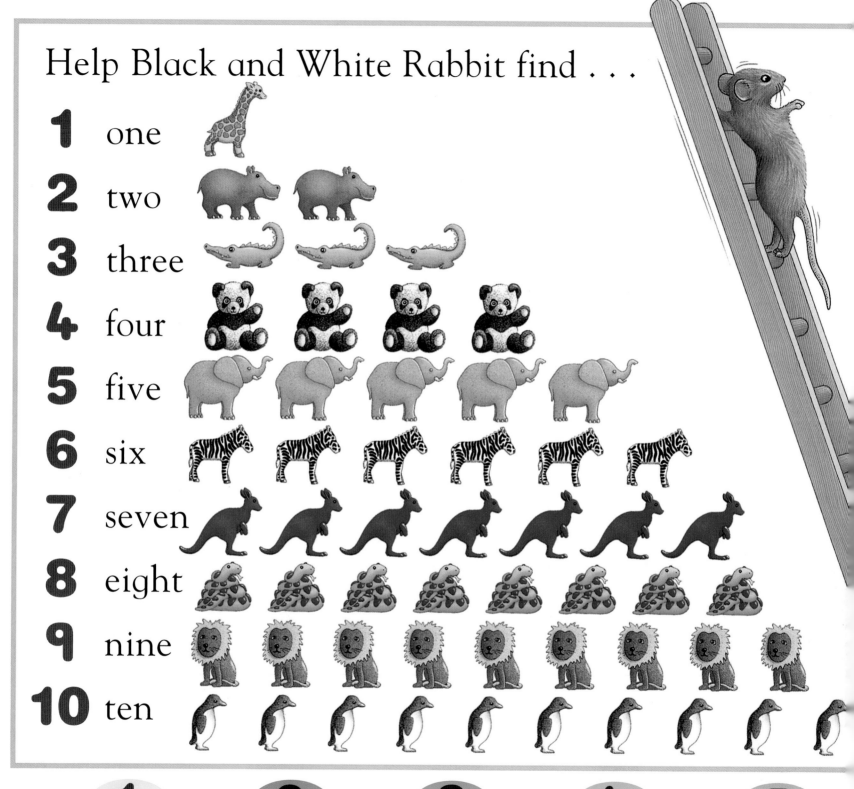

Help Black and White Rabbit find . . .

1 one

2 two

3 three

4 four

5 five

6 six

7 seven

8 eight

9 nine

10 ten

1 **2** **3** **4** **5**

6 7 8 9 10

9

How many wheels?

What has . . .

1 wheel? **2** wheels? **3** wheels?

4 wheels? **6** wheels?

8 wheels?

1 **2** **3** **4** **5**

Is there anything
that has no wheels?

Boats on the water

Count the boats with red sails.
Count the boats with yellow sails.
Can you find a boat with no sails?

1 2 3 4 5

How many boats have flags?

What does ten look like?

Ten of everything!
Use your fingers to help you count.

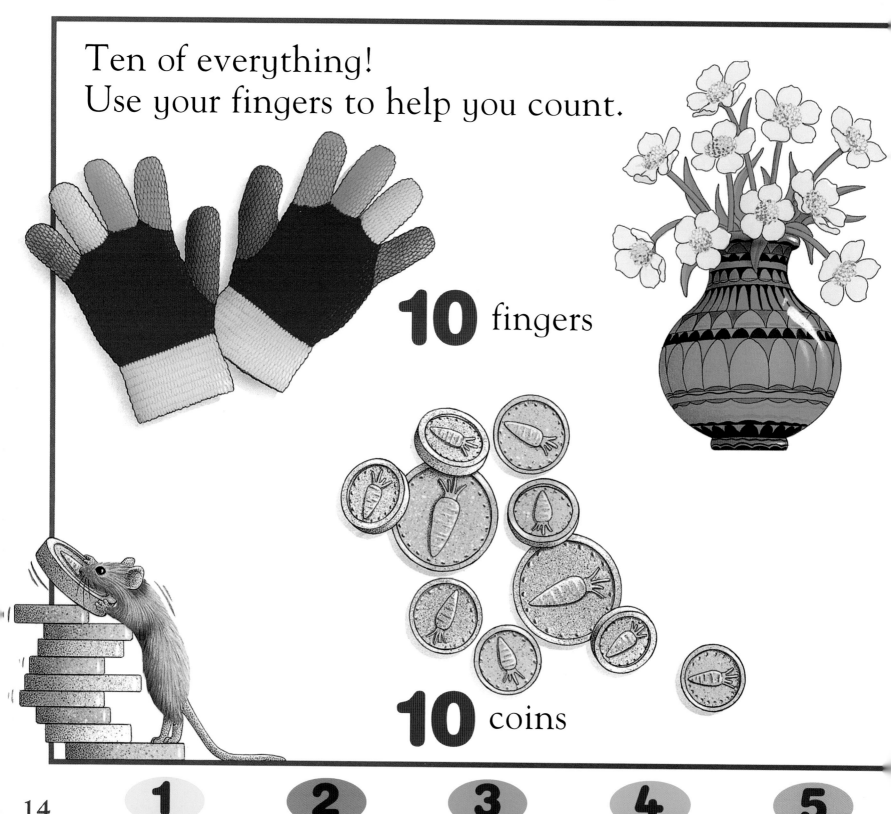

10 fingers

10 coins

1   2   3   4   5

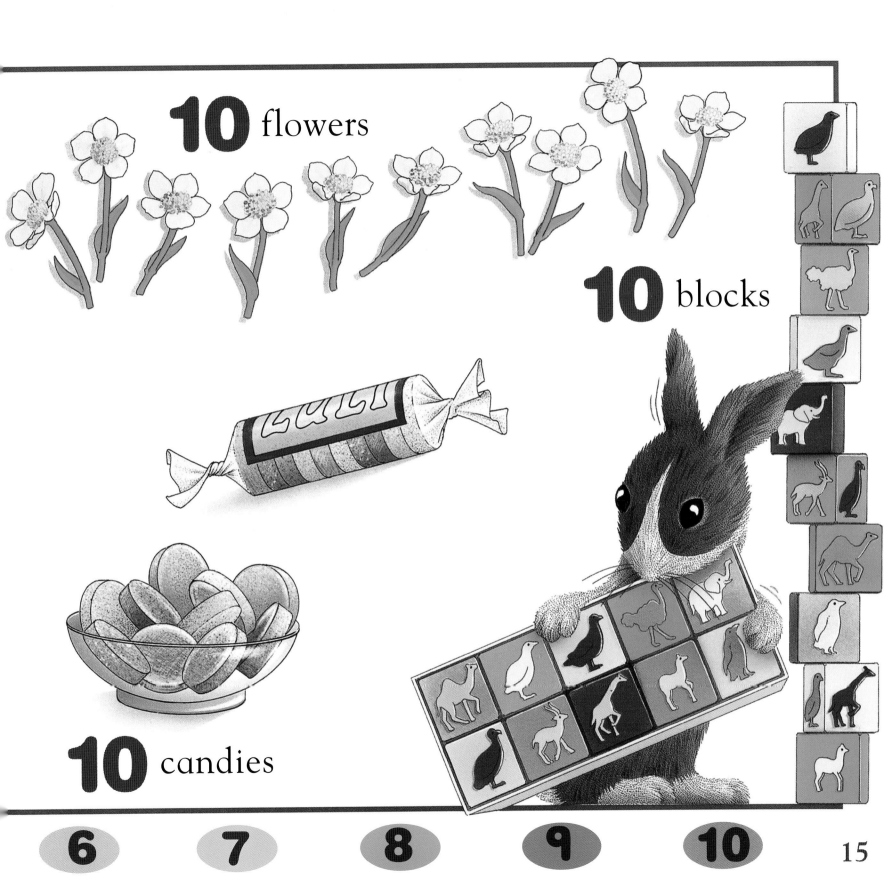

10 flowers

10 blocks

10 candies

6 7 8 9 10

Happy Birthday!

It's White Rabbit's birthday! How old is she?

How many rabbits have come to her party?

1 **2** **3** **4** **5**

How many balloons are there?
Can each rabbit take one home?

Is there a party
bag for everyone
at the party?

Here comes Mouse
with the juice.
Is there a glass for
everybody?

6 7 8 9 10

Shopping

Gray Rabbit is shopping for his favorite food.

Carrots
8¢ each

Onions
6¢ each

Potatoes
2¢ each

Tomatoes
7¢ each

1 **2** **3** **4** **5**

He brings along his pocket money.

How much does each carrot cost?

How many carrots are
in his basket?

How many bills is he
giving to Brown Rabbit?

Who has the most?

Which butterfly has the most spots?

Which rabbit has the fewest strawberries?

1 2 3 4 5

Does the red flower have fewer petals than the other flowers?

Does the centipede have more legs than the other creepy-crawlies?

Look who has eaten too much!

Pairs

Help White Rabbit match the pairs of socks.
How many pairs of socks are there?

1 2 3 4 5

How many pairs of shoes are there?
Can you see Mouse's other shoe?

Winning numbers

Which car is first?

Which car is second?

Which car is third?

24 **1** **2** **3** **4** **5**

And can you see who is last?

Finish

6 7 8 9 10

What comes after ten?

Gray Rabbit and Black and White Rabbit
are building tall towers.
What shape is on the tenth block?
Can you count all the way up to twenty?

eleven
11

twelve
12

thirteen
13

fourteen
14

fifteen
15

11 **12** **13** **14** **15**

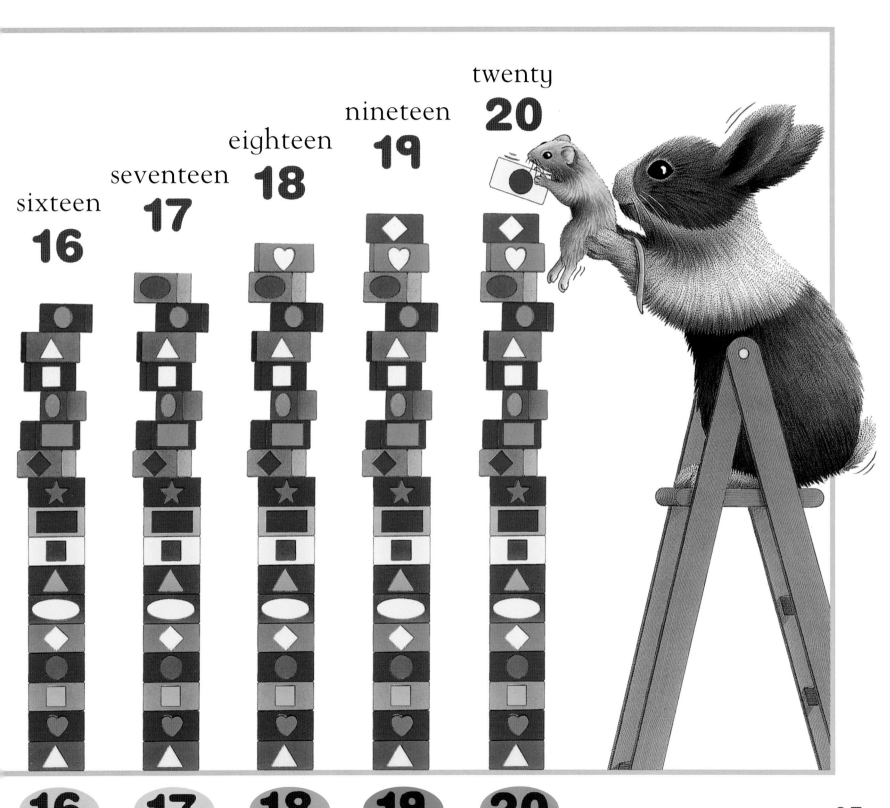

sixteen
16

seventeen
17

eighteen
18

nineteen
19

twenty
20

16 **17** **18** **19** **20**

More games to play

Playing games will further increase your child's confidence in using numbers. Here are some games to play with this book, plus ideas for playing with numbers in everyday life.

Giant number line

Draw the numbers 1 to 10 on paper plates. Mix up the plates, then help your child put them in order. Lay the plates in a sequential pattern (like hopscotch) on the floor so that your child can hop—literally—from one number to the next!

Mouse count

Ask your child to look for the little brown mouse that appears throughout the book. Count how many times Mouse appears. You can do the same with each of the rabbits. How many different rabbits are there?

Sort the socks

Ask your child to look again at White Rabbit's socks on pages 22 and 23. How many striped socks are there? How many with yellow on them? Play this game with real clothing, and talk about the different ways to sort—by type of clothing, by color, by pattern, etc.

Perfect pairs

Discuss things that come in pairs, such as 2 eyes, 2 ears, 2 hands, 2 feet. What else comes in twos?

Tiny shopper

Use real groceries for counting practice. Young children often find it easier to count real objects instead of pictures on a page. Your child can count the items in your shopping cart or play simple sorting games, such as putting cans into one pile and boxes into another. You can introduce the concept of money by using objects such as buttons or raisins as pretend coins.

5970 316

Big numbers, favorite numbers

Children love words that roll off the tongue. You can encourage your child to play with numbers in this way, too. Ask your child to think up a **really** big number. Even if it is nonsensical like "ninety-twenty-thousand-hundred," you can talk about it to help your child understand the order of bigger numbers—thousands are bigger than hundreds, for example.

Numbers everywhere

Look out for numbers in the world around you—and help your child to enjoy applying their newly found number skills.

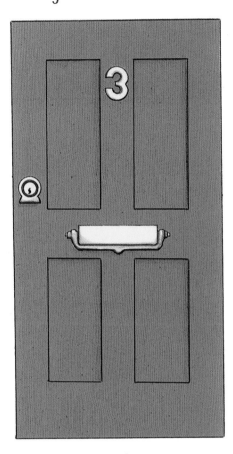

6 **7** **8** **9** **10**